Presents

Reading Music for
GUITAR

An Easy To Follow Method For Reading Music

Written & Method By:
John McCarthy

Adapted By: Jimmy Rutkowski
Supervising Editor: John McCarthy
Music Transcribing & Engraving: Jimmy Rutkowski
Production Manager: John McCarthy
Layout, Graphics & Design: Jimmy Rutkowski
Photography: Rodney Dabney, Jimmy Rutkowski
Copy Editors: Cathy McCarthy

Cover Art Direction & Design:
Jimmy Rutkowski

HL00110200
ISBN: 978-1-4768 -7421-0

Table of Contents

Words from the Author

Playing guitar is a rewarding art form that will last you a lifetime. I have spent my career sharing the passion I have for guitar with others. If you follow my guitar method step-by-step you will be successful and enjoy playing guitar for years to come. When I designed The Rock House Method, my mission was to create the most complete, easy and fun way to learn. I accomplished this by developing and systematically arranging a modern method based on the needs and social demands of today's players. I believe every musician should learn the language of music that is universal, music notation. In this book I will guide you through the process of learning to read music in a modern and fun manner. I not only tell you where to put your fingers, but I will show you ways to use what you learn so that you can make music right from the start. As you progress as a guitar player, keep your mind open to all styles of music. Set up a practice schedule that you can manage, be consistent, challenge yourself and realize everyone learns at a different rate. Be patient, persistent and remember music is supposed to be fun!

Now, GET EXCITED! YOU are going to play guitar!

John McCarthy

Digital eBook

When you register this product at the Lesson Support site RockHouseSchool.com, you will receive a digital version of this book. This interactive eBook can be used on all devices that support Adobe PDF. This will allow you to access your book using the latest portable technology any time you want.

Register using the member number found **on the CD** in the back of the book.

The Rock House Method Learning System

This learning system can be used on your own or guided by a teacher. Be sure to register for your free lesson support at RockHouseSchool.com. Your member number can be found inside the cover of this book.

Lesson Support Site: Once registered, you can use this fully interactive site along with your product to enhance your learning experience, expand your knowledge, link with instructors and connect with a community of people around the world who are learning to play music using The Rock House Method®.

Quick Start Video: The quick start video is designed to guide you through your first steps! All the basic information you will need to get playing now is demonstrated.

Gear Education Video: Walking into a music store can be an intimidating endeavor for someone starting out. To help you, Rock House has a series of videos to educate you on some of the gear you will encounter as you start your musical journey.

Care Video: This video will help you with the care and maintenance of your instrument. From changing strings to cleaning your guitar, learn many helpful tips.

Quizzes: Each level of the curriculum contains multiple quizzes to gauge your progress. When you see a quiz icon go to the *Lesson Support* site and take the quiz. It will be graded and emailed to you for review.

Audio Examples & Play Along Tracks: Demonstrations of how each lesson should sound and full band backing tracks to play certain lessons over. These audio tracks are available on the accompanying mp3 CD.

Icon Key

These tell you there is additional information and learning utilities available at RockHouseSchool.com to support that lesson.

Backing Track

CD Track Backing track icons are placed on lessons where there is an audio demonstration to let you hear what that lesson should sound like or a backing track to play the lesson over. Use these audio tracks to guide you through the lessons. **This is an mp3 CD, it can be played on any computer and all mp3 disc compatible playback devices.**

Metronome

A metronome is a device that clicks at an adjustable rate that you set. It is a great way to gauge your progress when learning a song, scale or exercise. Metronome icons are placed next to the examples that we recommend you practice using a metronome. You can download a free, adjustable metronome on the *Lesson Support* site.

Worksheet

Worksheets are a great tool to help you thoroughly learn and understand music. These worksheets can be downloaded at the *Lesson Support* site.

Tuner

You can download the free online tuner on the *Lesson Support* site to help tune your instrument.

The Staff

Music is written on a **STAFF** consisting of **FIVE LINES** and **FOUR SPACES**. The lines and spaces are numbered as shown:

5th Line ──────────────────────────────
        4th Space
4th Line ──────────────────────────────
        3rd Space
3rd Line ──────────────────────────────
        2nd Space
2nd Line ──────────────────────────────
        1st Space
1st Line ──────────────────────────────

The lines and spaces are named after letters of the alphabet. You can use this saying to memorize the names easily. The lines are named as follows:

5 ───────────────────(F)───   Fine
4 ──────────────(D)──────   Does
3 ────────(B)────────────   Boy
2 ──────(G)──────────────   Good
1 ───(E)──────────────── Every

The letter names of the spaces are F – A – C – E they spell the word "FACE."

4 ──────────────────────E──
3 ────────────────C────────
2 ──────────A──────────────
1 ──────F──────────────────

F-A-C-E

The Musical Alphabet

The musical alphabet consists of seven letters A through G. After G the letters loop back to A and start over again. There are no note names higher in the musical alphabet then G.

A - B - C - D - E - F - G

Staff Symbols

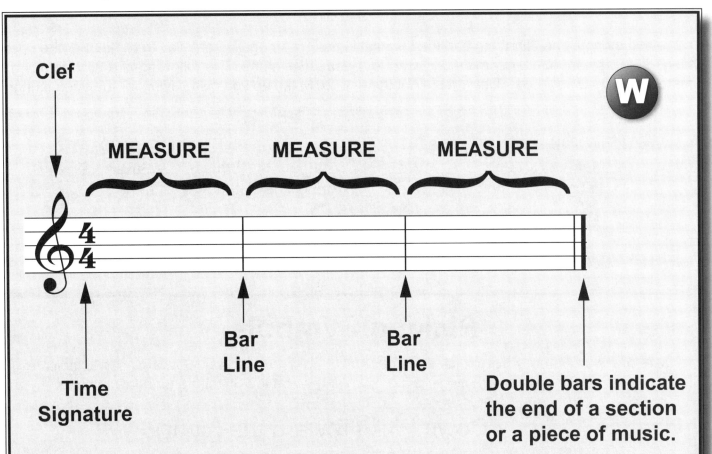

Measures & Bar Lines

The staff is divided into measures by vertical lines called bar lines.

Treble Clef

The second line of the treble clef is known as the G line. Some people call the treble clef the "G clef" because the tail circles around the G line of the staff.

Time Signature

Time signatures are written at the beginning of a piece of music. The top number tells you how many beats there are in each measure and the bottom number tells what type of beat is receiving the count.

4 = Number of beats per measure.

4 = A Quarter note receiving one beat.

Names of the Open Strings & Tuning

CD Track
2

The fattest string is the 6th string and the thinnest is the 1st string. A great way to remember the open strings is to use an acronym creating a word for each letter name. The following is a silly acronym I created: Every – Bad – Girl – Deserves – Another – Egg. Make up you own saying for the open strings.

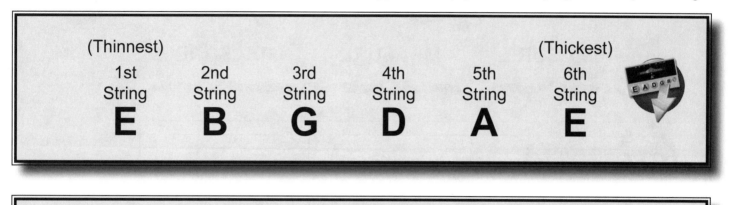

(Thinnest)					(Thickest)
1st String	2nd String	3rd String	4th String	5th String	6th String
E	**B**	**G**	**D**	**A**	**E**

Picking Symbols

There are two different ways to pick a string: down or up. The symbols below are used to indicate a down pick or an up pick. Practice picking down and up on the 6th string for a few minutes.

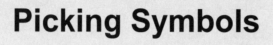

⊓ = Down Pick (Toward the Floor)

∨ = Up Pick (Toward the Ceiling)

An easy way of remembering which symbol is which in the beginning, is to realize that the open side of each symbol is in the direction of the pick stroke that it represents.

Counting Beats

A beat is the basic unit of time in music. A common way to count beats is to tap your foot. One beat would equal tapping your foot down-up. Tap your foot and count 1 – 2 – 3 – 4 repetitively, say each number as your foot hits the ground. Next you will learn different note types that tell you how many beats to let notes ring.

Foot Down

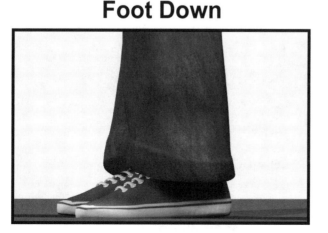

Foot Up

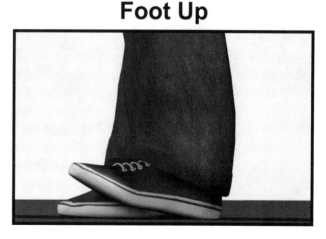

Music Notes

The Parts of a Note

The HEAD

The STEM

The FLAG

The Types of Notes

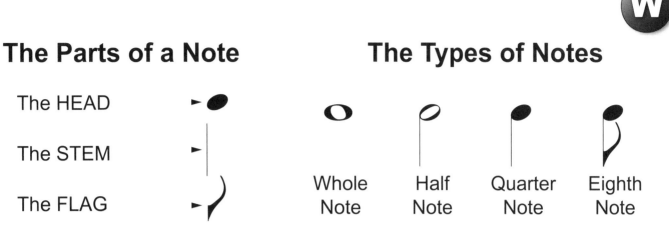

Whole Note   Half Note   Quarter Note   Eighth Note

Whole Notes = 4 Beats

This is a Whole Note. The head is hollow and there is no stem or flag. A Whole Note will receive four beats or counts. Pick the open 6th string and let it ring for 4 beats.

Half Notes = 2 Beats

This is a Half Note. The head is hollow and there is a stem. A Half Note will receive two beats or counts. Pick the open 6th string on beats 1 and 3.

Quarter Notes = 1 Beat

This is a Quarter Note. The head is solid and there is a stem. A Quarter Note will receive one beat or count. Pick the 6th string on every beat.

First String Notes

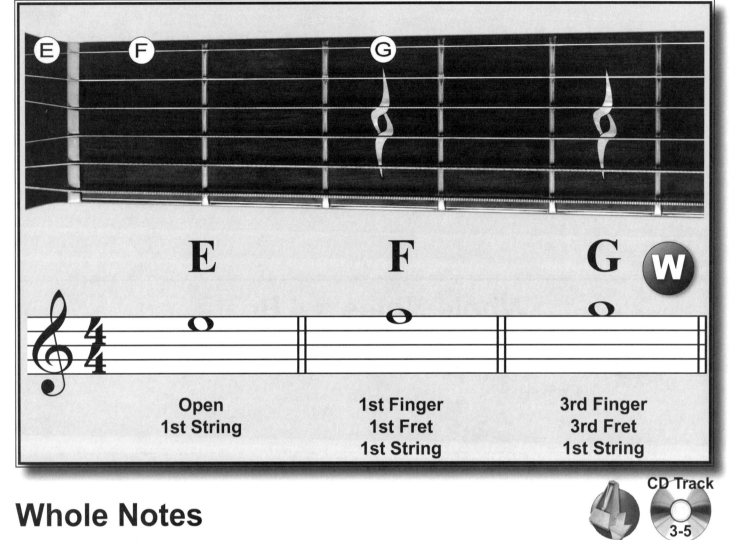

Open 1st String — E
1st Finger 1st Fret 1st String — F
3rd Finger 3rd Fret 1st String — G

CD Track 3-5

Whole Notes

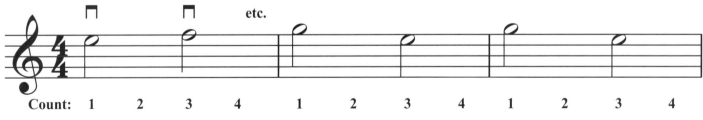

Count: 1 2 3 4 1 2 3 4 1 2 3 4 1 2 3 4 1 2 3 4 1 2 3 4 1 2 3 4 1 2 3 4

Half Notes

Count: 1 2 3 4 1 2 3 4 1 2 3 4

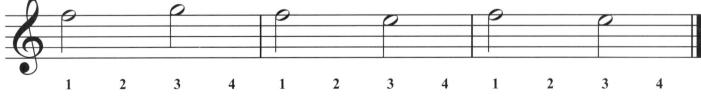

1 2 3 4 1 2 3 4 1 2 3 4

Quarter Notes

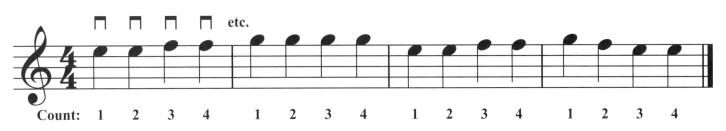

Count: 1 2 3 4   1 2 3 4   1 2 3 4   1 2 3 4

Rests

A rest is a period of silence. Like whole, half and quarter notes you keep time only there is no sound. See what each rest looks like below:

Whole Note Rest	Half Note Rest	Quarter Note Rest
4 Beats	2 Beats	1 Beat

Lesson Accompaniment

Throughout this book certain songs will have letters above the staff like the song below. These are chords that a teacher can strum as you play the song. You can also find a backing track of these chords to practice along with on the accompanying CD.

1st String Etude

CD Track 6-7

Count: 1 2 3 4   1 2 3 4

Second String Notes

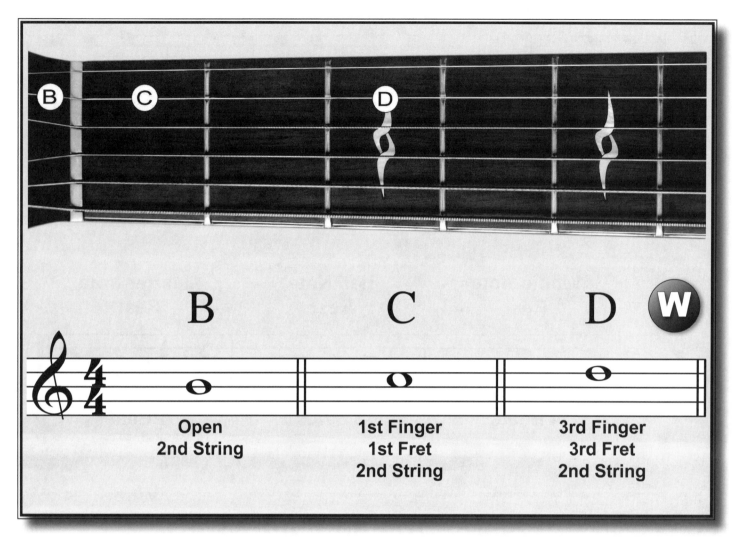

2nd String Etude

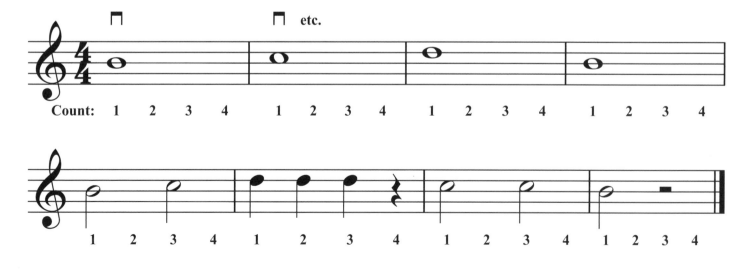

Hot Cross Buns

CD Track 9-10

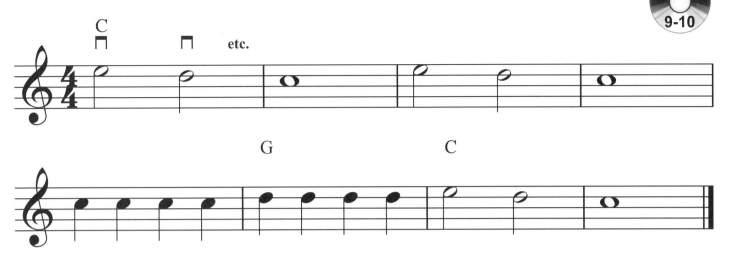

By the Sil'very Moonlight

CD Track 11-12

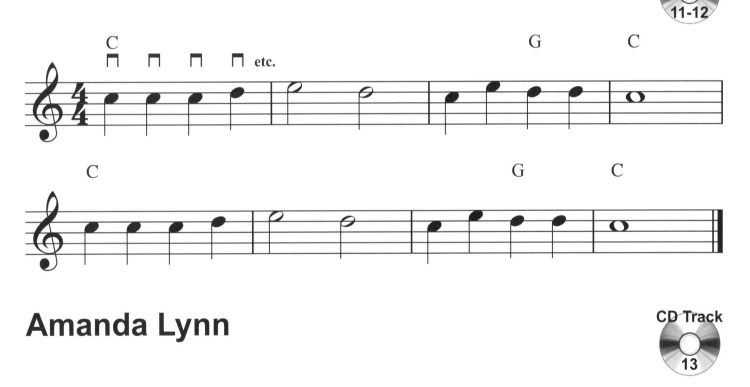

Amanda Lynn

CD Track 13

Good King Wenceslas

CD Track 14-15

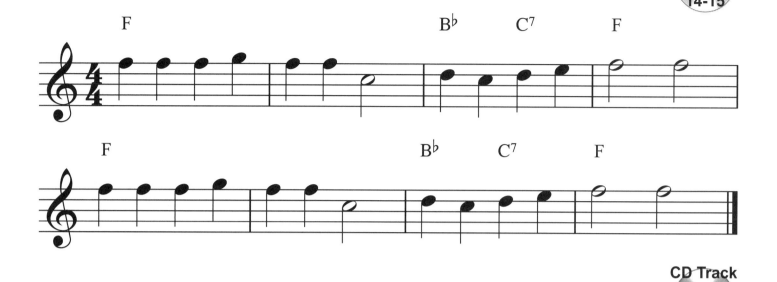

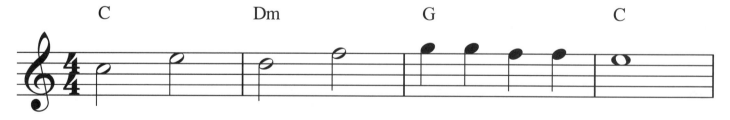

Go Tell Aunt Rhody

CD Track 16-17

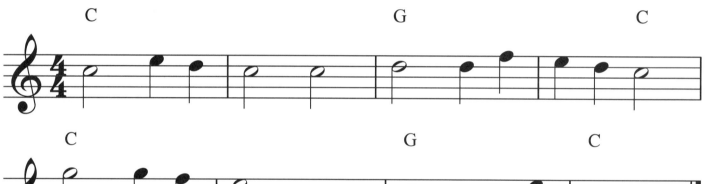

Two String Combo

CD Track 18-19

Pick Up Notes

When there is an incomplete measure starting a song these notes are called "pick up notes." When this occurs the last measure will also be incomplete; but, the combination of both together will equal a full measure. When counting into the song still count the full count but just start earlier.

Count: 1   2   3   4

A Tisket, A Tasket

CD Track
20-21

Dotted Half Notes

A dotted half note receives three beats or counts. It is a regular half note with a dot placed after it. The dotted half note will be used in the next song.

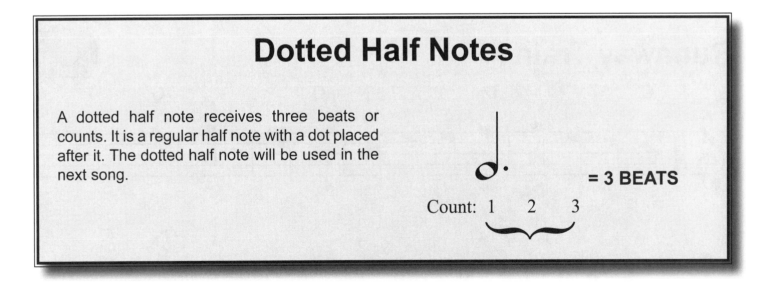

= 3 BEATS

15

3/4 Timing

Here is a new time signature that will be used in the next song. In 3/4 time there are three beats per measure. This timing is used in many songs.

I Saw Three Ships

CD Track 22-23

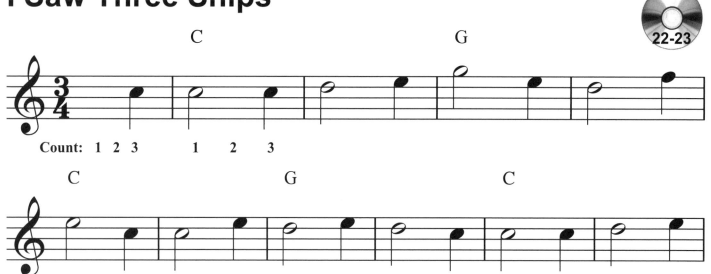

Count: 1 2 3   1 2 3

Count: 1 2 3

Runaway Train

CD Track 24-25

Third & Fourth String Notes

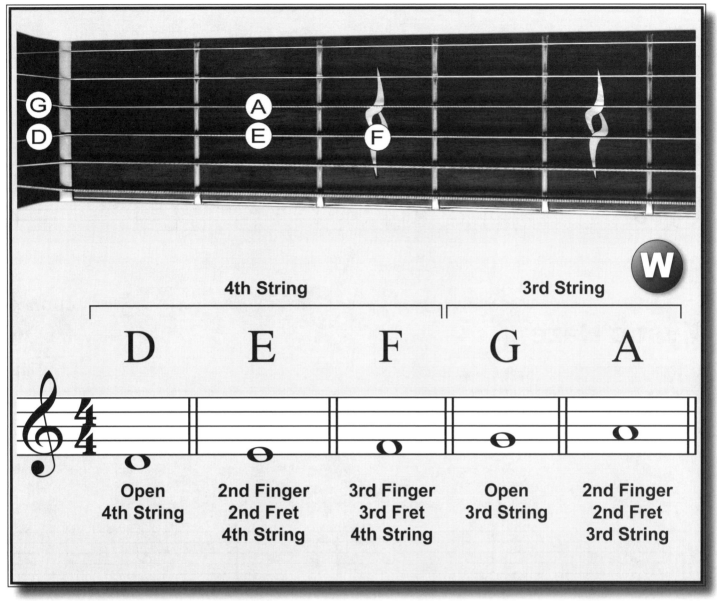

3rd & 4th String Etude

CD Track 26

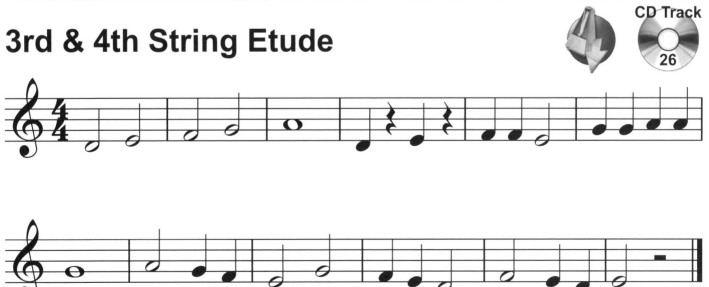

Aura Lee

CD Track 27-28

Mystic Haze

CD Track 29

Johnny Blues

CD Track 30-31

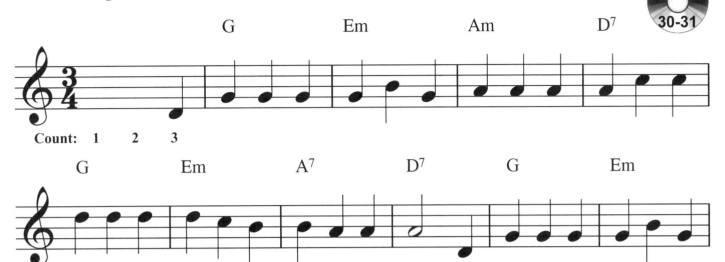

Count: 1 2 3

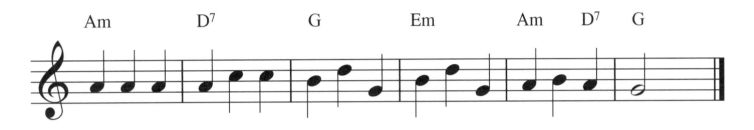

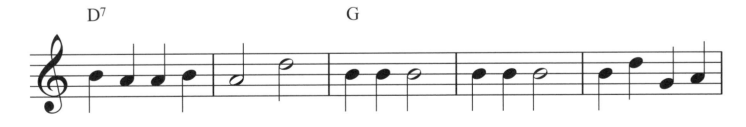

Rockin the Bells

CD Track 32-33

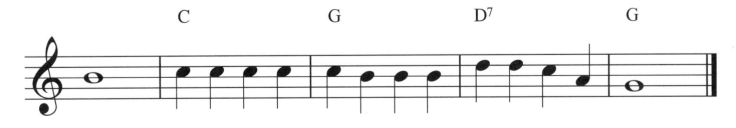

The Tie

When notes on the **same** line or space are joined with a curved line, they are called tied notes. The note is only played once but will ring for the combined values of both notes.

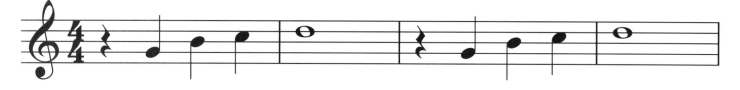

Count: 1 2 3 4   1 2 3 4

Oh When the Saints

CD Track
34-35

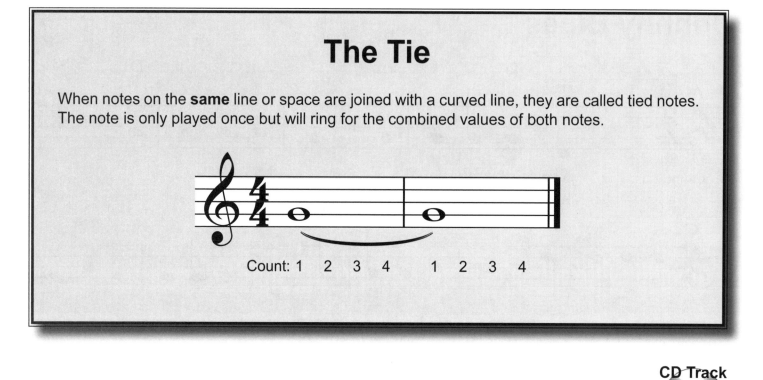

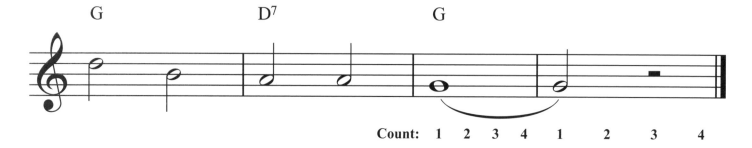

Count: 1 2 3 4 1 2 3 4

The High A Note

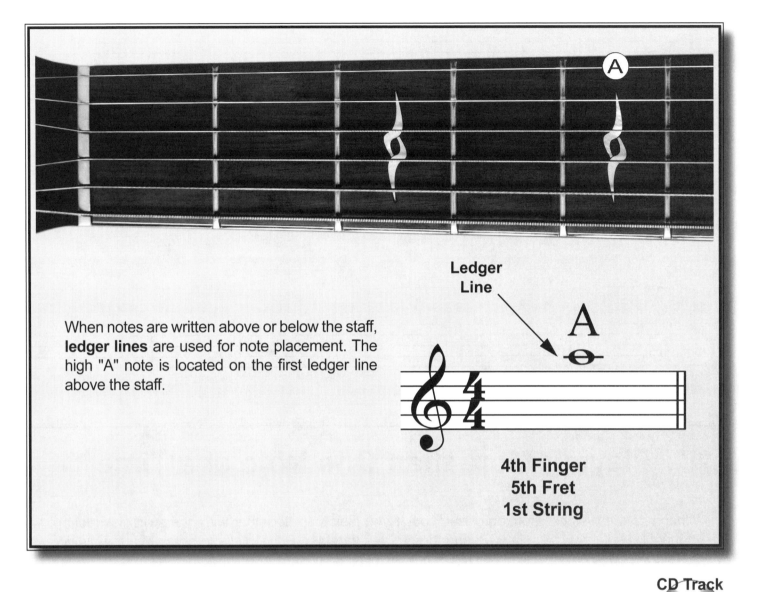

When notes are written above or below the staff, **ledger lines** are used for note placement. The high "A" note is located on the first ledger line above the staff.

Ledger Line

A

4th Finger
5th Fret
1st String

Bottoms Up

CD Track
36-37

21

Amazing Grace

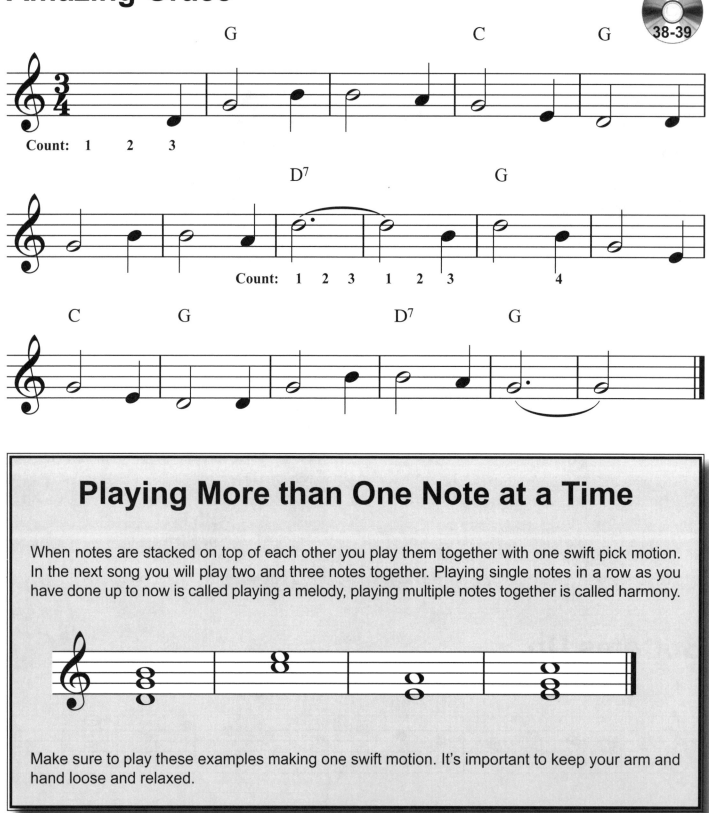

Playing More than One Note at a Time

When notes are stacked on top of each other you play them together with one swift pick motion. In the next song you will play two and three notes together. Playing single notes in a row as you have done up to now is called playing a melody, playing multiple notes together is called harmony.

Make sure to play these examples making one swift motion. It's important to keep your arm and hand loose and relaxed.

Reading Music for Guitar - Quiz 1

Once you complete this section go to RockHouseSchool.com and take the Quiz to track your progress. You will receive an email with your results and suggestions.

Surprise Symphony

CD Track 40-41

We Three Kings

CD Track 42-43

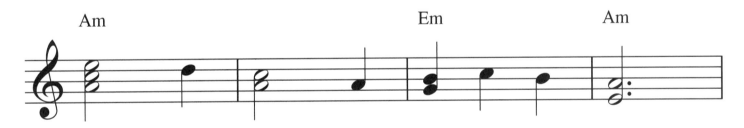

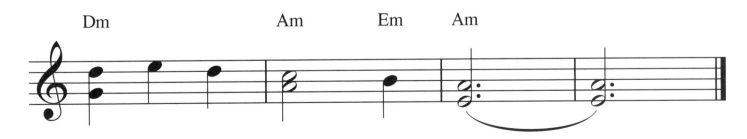

Simile Marks

Simile marks tell you to repeat the measure before. When you see this mark in a song play the measure before it then continue through the rest of the song as written. In the next song you will use simile marks.

Double Down

Jolly Old Saint Nick

Fifth & Sixth String Notes

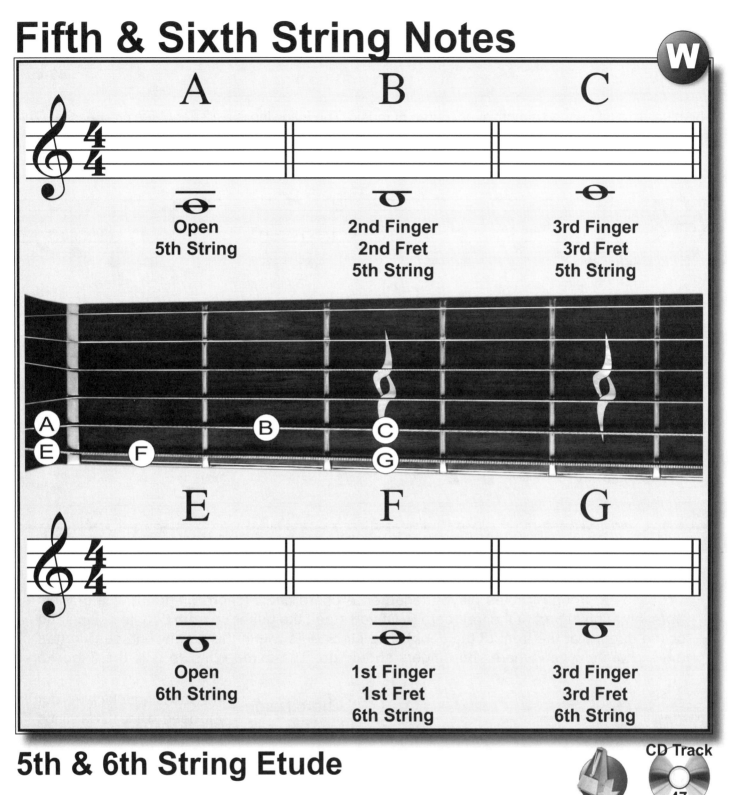

5th & 6th String Etude

CD Track
47

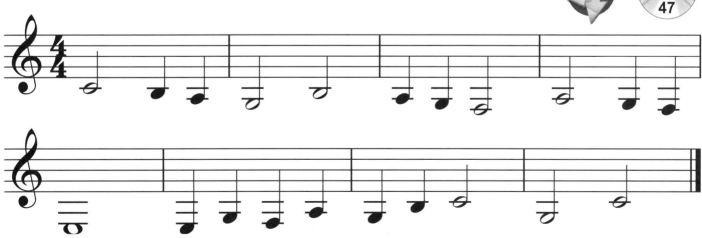

12 Bar Blues

The blues has influenced almost every genre of music. The following is a 12 bar blues progression. This means there is 12 measures of music. This 12 measure structure repeats throughout a song.

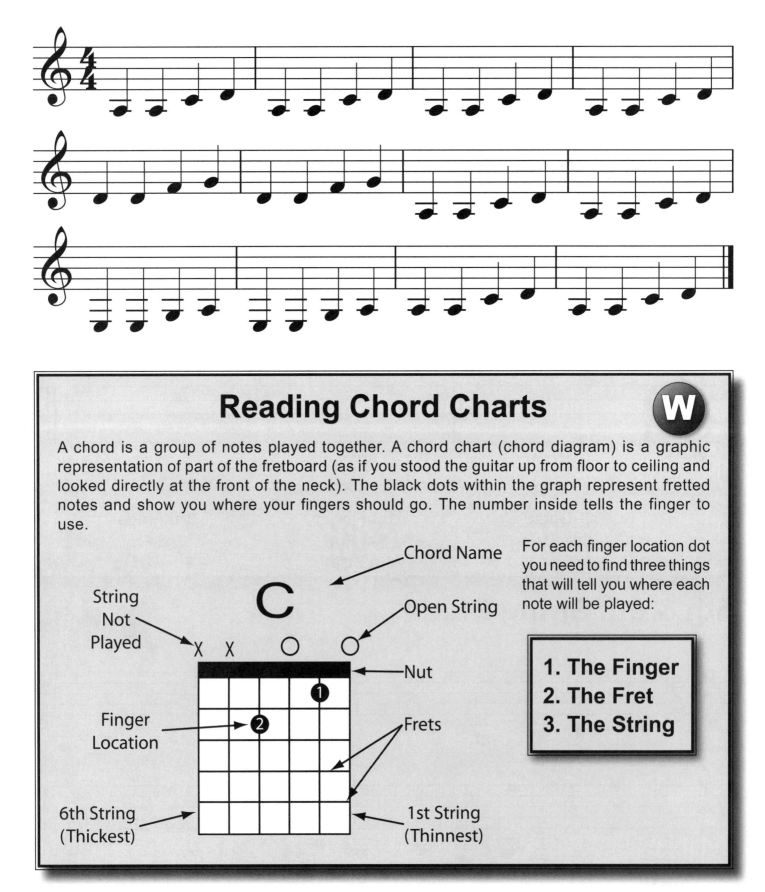

Reading Chord Charts

A chord is a group of notes played together. A chord chart (chord diagram) is a graphic representation of part of the fretboard (as if you stood the guitar up from floor to ceiling and looked directly at the front of the neck). The black dots within the graph represent fretted notes and show you where your fingers should go. The number inside tells the finger to use.

Chord Name

String Not Played

Open String

Nut

Finger Location

Frets

6th String (Thickest)

1st String (Thinnest)

For each finger location dot you need to find three things that will tell you where each note will be played:

1. The Finger
2. The Fret
3. The String

Your First Chords

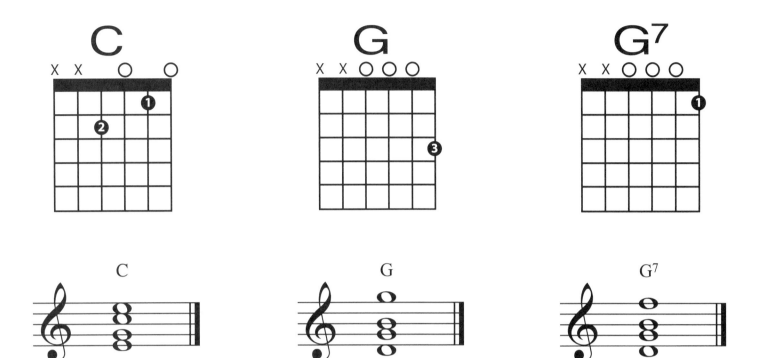

Strumming Chords

CD Track

50-52

To strum chords pivot your arm from the elbow and rake the pick across the strings in one swift motion. For the examples in this lesson you will use all down strums. Be sure to keep your arm loose and relaxed. There are three variations using whole, half and quarter note strumming. Play these progressions over the bass and drum backing track and feel how it is to play with a full band.

Whole Note Strums

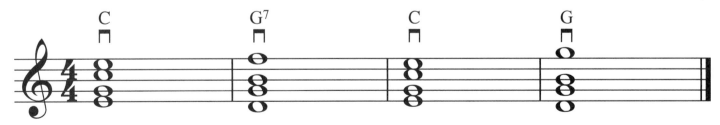

Half Note Strums

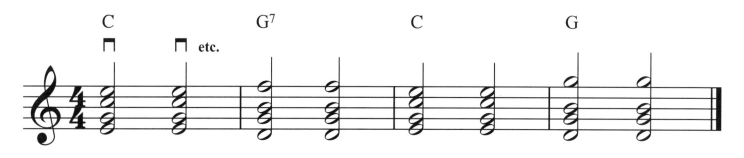

Quarter Note Strums

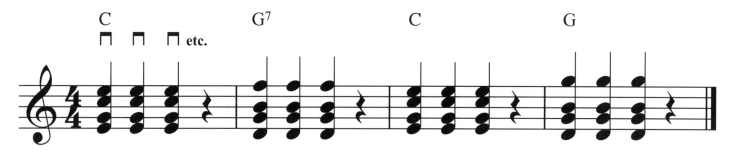

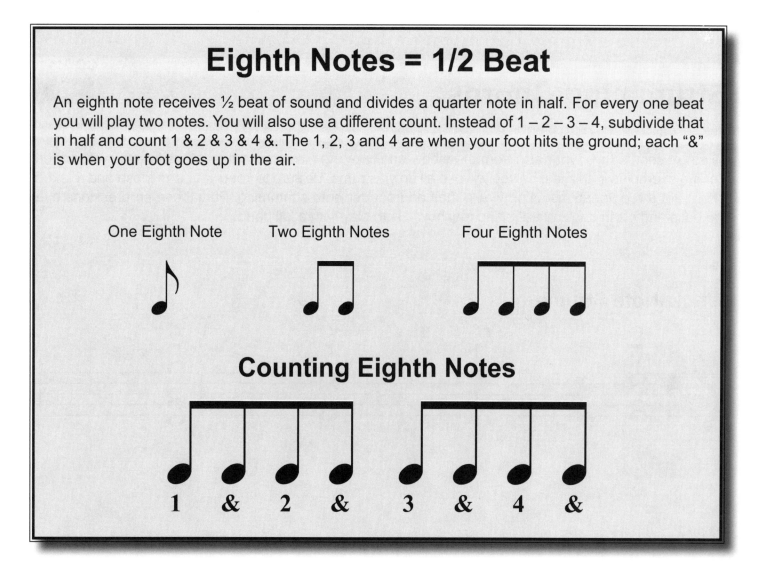

Eighth Notes = 1/2 Beat

An eighth note receives ½ beat of sound and divides a quarter note in half. For every one beat you will play two notes. You will also use a different count. Instead of 1 – 2 – 3 – 4, subdivide that in half and count 1 & 2 & 3 & 4 &. The 1, 2, 3 and 4 are when your foot hits the ground; each "&" is when your foot goes up in the air.

One Eighth Note   Two Eighth Notes   Four Eighth Notes

Counting Eighth Notes

1 & 2 & 3 & 4 &

Two for One

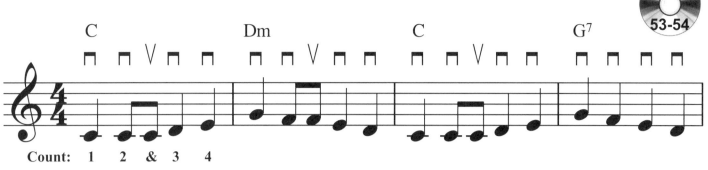

Count: 1   2   &   3   4

My Melody

The Arkansas Traveler

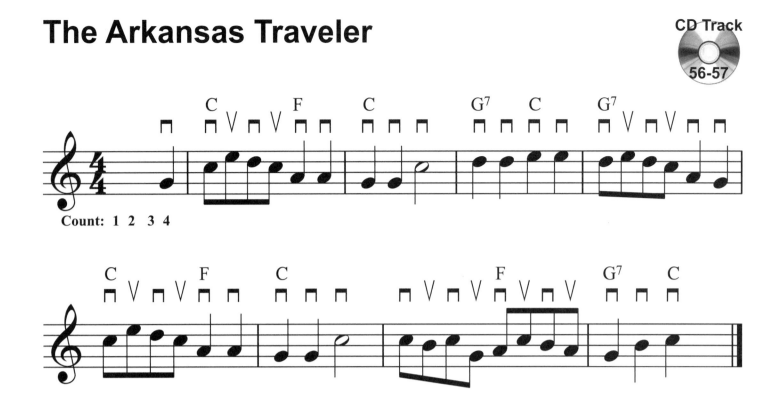

Count: 1 2 3 4

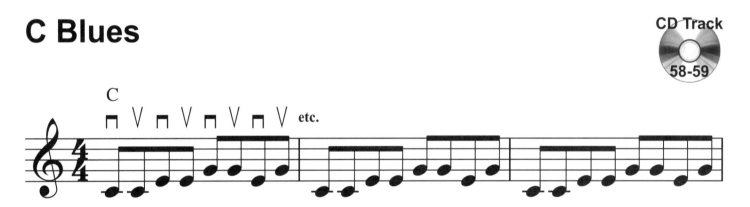

C Blues

Tempo

Tempo is the speed in which music is played. It is measured in beats per minute or bpm. There will be a tempo setting at the beginning of many songs that require a specific tempo. Here are some of the most common tempo settings.

Adagio - Slow -66 - 76 bpm

Andante - Moderately Slow 76 - 108 bpm

Moderato - Moderate - 108 - 120 bpm

Allegro - Fast - 120 - 168 bpm

CD Track
60

Beethoven's 5th

Allegro

The Notes in the First Position

The first position on the guitar is the first four frets. The notes you have learned so far on all six strings are the notes in the first position. It is important to memorize these notes because you will be learning songs throughout the rest of this book using these notes.

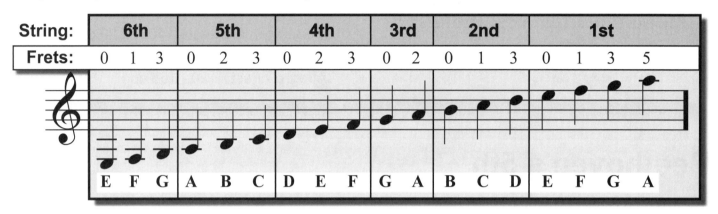

String:	6th			5th			4th			3rd		2nd			1st			
Frets:	0	1	3	0	2	3	0	2	3	0	2	0	1	3	0	1	3	5
	E	F	G	A	B	C	D	E	F	G	A	B	C	D	E	F	G	A

Hitting All Six

CD Track 61

Moderato

32

The C Major Scale

The notes that form the C major scale are C – D – E – F – G – A – B – C. Scales will be used to make melodies, riffs and complete songs.

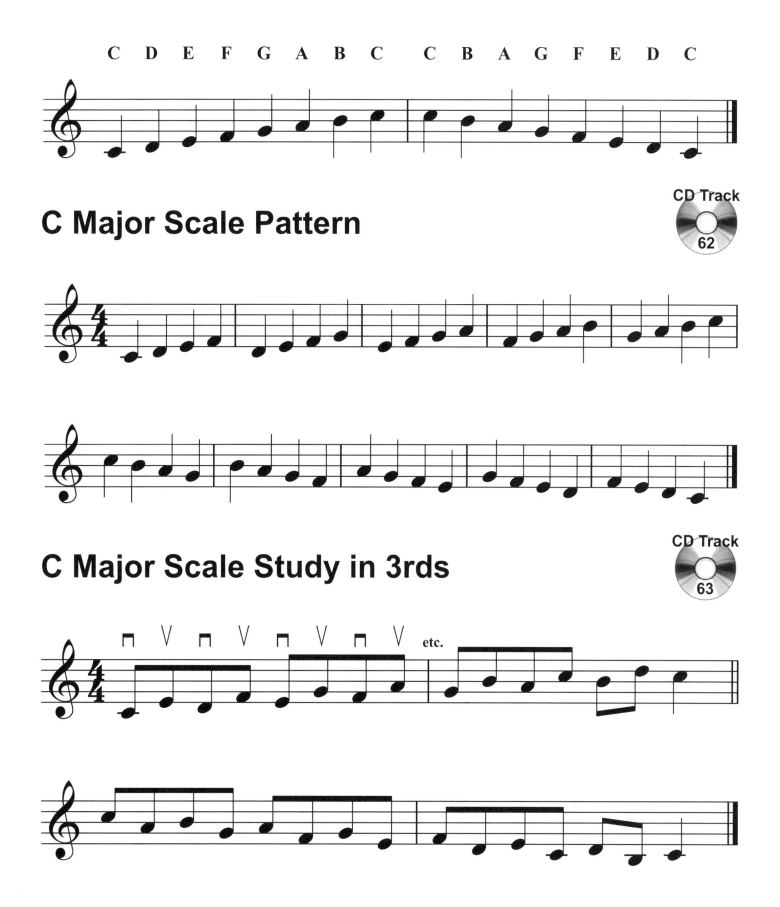

C Major Scale Pattern

CD Track 62

C Major Scale Study in 3rds

CD Track 63

Full Form Chords

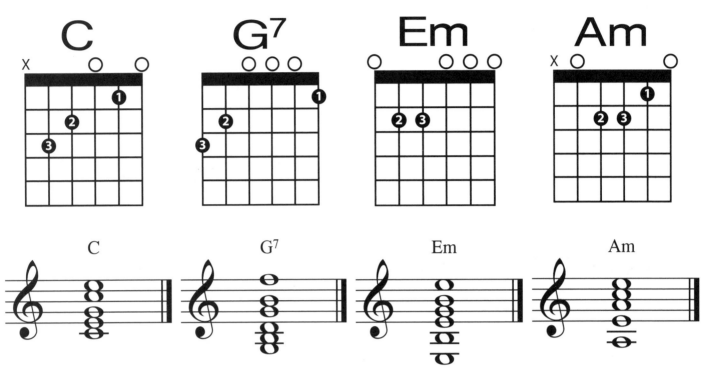

Rhythm Notation Chord Strum Slashes

Songs are created when you combine chords together to form progressions. Rhythm notation will be used in this book to show you how to strum each chord. The note values you learned will indicate the rhythm to strum each chord. The basic appearance of each note type will be the same but with a slightly different shape.

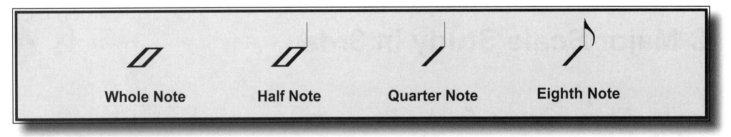

| Whole Note | Half Note | Quarter Note | Eighth Note |

The following is an example of a rhythm chord progression. The chord names are written above the staff, and the rhythm notation indicates the rhythm in which the chords are strummed.

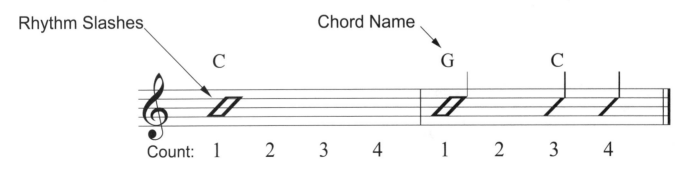

Repeat Sign Brackets

A repeat sign is a sign that indicates a section of music that should be repeated. If the piece has one repeat sign alone, then that means to repeat from the beginning, and then continue on (or stop, if the sign appears at the end of the piece). A repeat sign facing the other way indicates where the repeat is to begin and the music between the two bars is to be repeated.

Repeat all measures between brackets

Song Chord Progressions

Progression 1

Progression 2

Progression 3

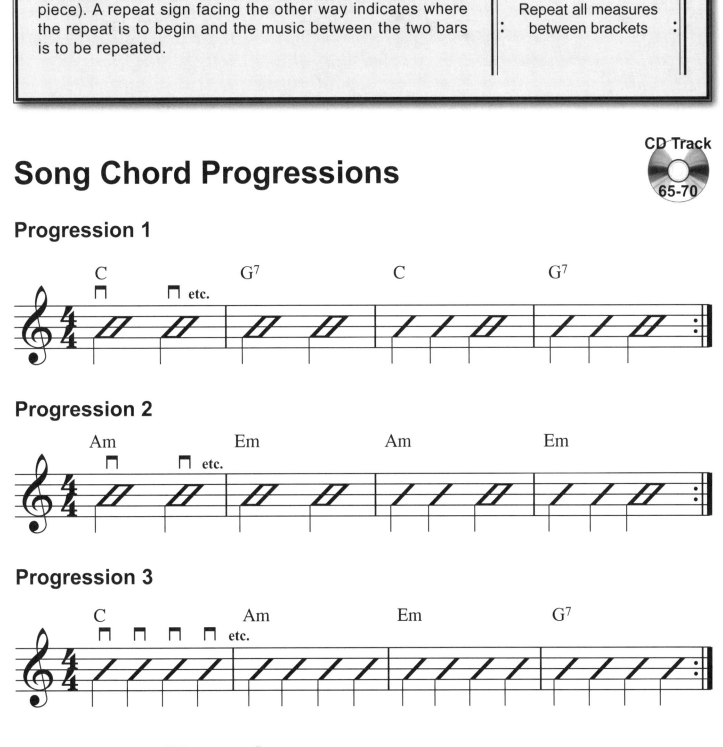

Alternate Fingerings

At times to play songs effectively you will need to use alternate fingerings. This will help position your hand to play sections with ease. These alternate fingering will be depicted with numbers placed next to the note. Take notice in the next song, "Canon", there will be some alternate fingerings used.

Canon

Andante

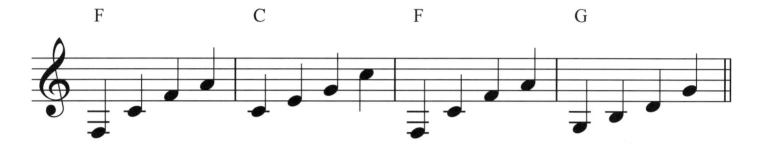

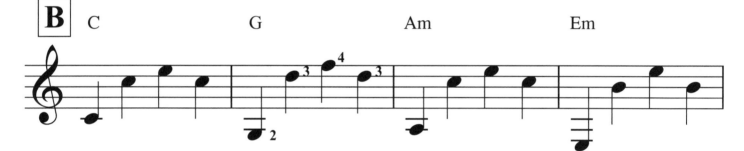

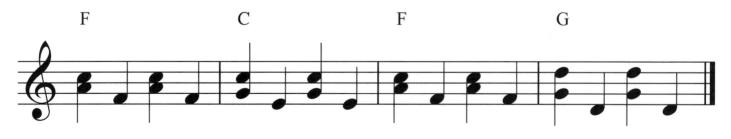

Rehearsal Marks

Rehearsal marks allow you to quickly navigate to a specific point in a song; this will help you to master more difficult passages when practicing. Even after the piece has been mastered, rehearsal marks continue to provide location signposts helping you to stay oriented during performances. In the preceding song the rehearsal marks designated the three movements of Canon with an A, B and C.

CD Track

73-80

Bass Note Strum Studies

In the following exercises you will hold down a chord, pick the bass note then strum the upper register of the chord to form a rhythm. This technique allows you to play bass notes and rhythm chord strums in one progression. Be aware of the chord changes above the staff and fret the complete chord before playing each measure. Take note that each measure has two complete parts and timing, one for the bass notes and one for the strum.

Example 1 - Whole Note Bass

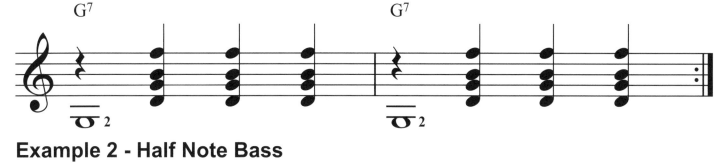

Example 2 - Half Note Bass

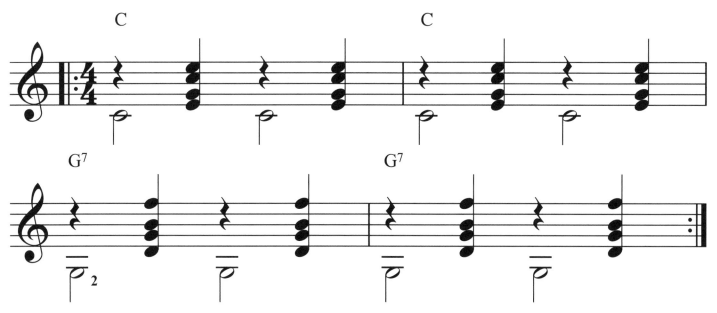

Example 3 - 3/4 Timing

Example 4 - Alternating Bass

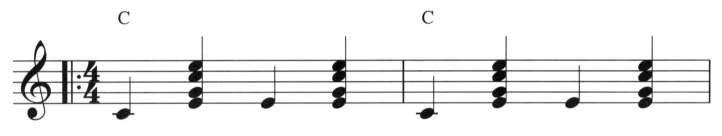

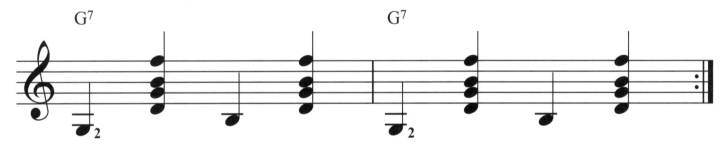

Dynamics in Music

As you are playing a song there will often be symbols that tell you what dynamic level to play the song. The dynamic level is how loud or soft the song should be played. The following are the symbols used for dynamics.

p - Piano, meaning soft

mp - Mezzo-piano, meaning medium soft

mf - Mezzo-forte, meaning medium loud

f - Forte, meaning loud

This Land is Your Land

Moderato

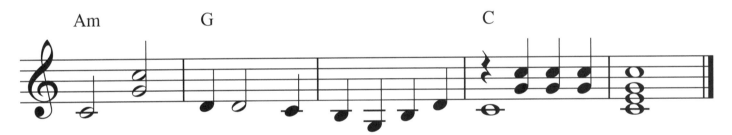

Dotted Quarter Notes

A dotted quarter note has a solid head with a dot next to it and a stem. The dotted quarter note receives 1 1/2 beats (counts).

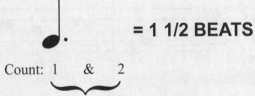

= 1 1/2 BEATS

Count: 1 & 2

Dotted quarter notes are often followed by eighth notes to make an even two beats. Below are a series of dotted quarter and eighth notes. Play and count these out loud:

1 & 2 & 3 & 4 &   1 & 2 & 3 & 4 &

Kum-Ba-Ya

Allegro

CD Track 83-84

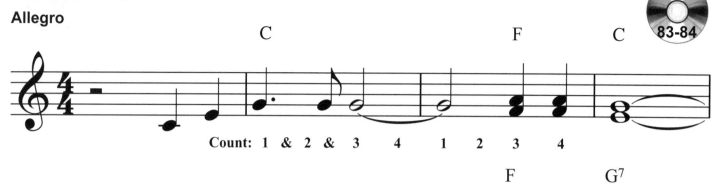

Count: 1 & 2 & 3 4 1 2 3 4

The New Years Song

CD Track 85-86

Moderato

Count: 1 2 3 4

Using the Metronome to Practice

As you progress as a guitarist you can use the metronome in your daily practice to help keep a steady rhythm and gauge your progress. Here are a few metronome practice tips that will help you use this tool effectively.

1. When starting to learn a new song set the metronome at a slow tempo where you can play the entire piece through without making mistakes.

2. Gradually build your speed by increasing the BPM (beats per minute) on the metronome a few numbers each day.

3. As you play with the metronome try not to focus on it too much. Sense the feel of the click and concentrate on the song you are playing.

Finger Flexing #1

CD Track 87

Ode to Joy

Andante

My Country tis of Thee

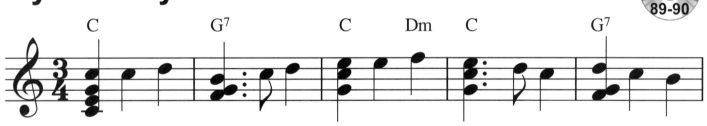

Triplet Timing

Eighth notes subdivide a beat in half. This is an even number breakdown. Triplets subdivide a beat into threes. For every one beat, you're going to play three notes. Count triplets like this:

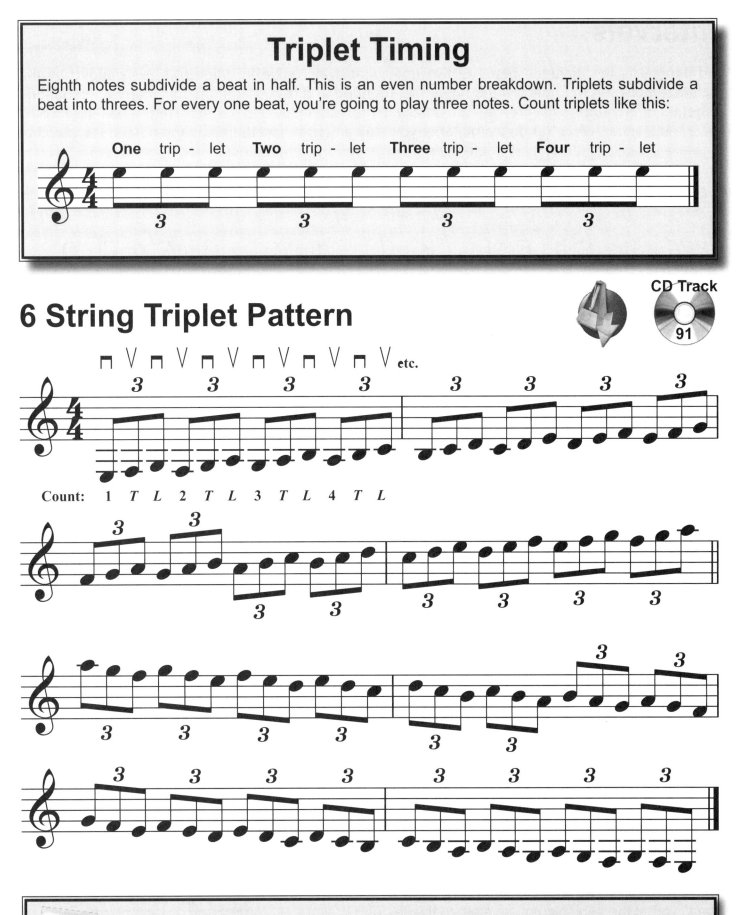

6 String Triplet Pattern

CD Track 91

Count: 1 T L 2 T L 3 T L 4 T L

Reading Music for Guitar - Quiz 2
Once you complete this section go to RockHouseSchool.com and take the Quiz to track your progress. You will receive an email with your results and suggestions.

Intervals

An interval is the distance between two notes. Intervals come in different sizes gauged by the distance between the notes. If the notes are sounded in a row, it is a melodic interval. If sounded together, it is a harmonic interval. The smallest interval in music is the half step. A half step would be the distance of one fret on the guitar. If you play any note and then play the note at the next fret you are playing a half step. A whole step is made up of two half steps.

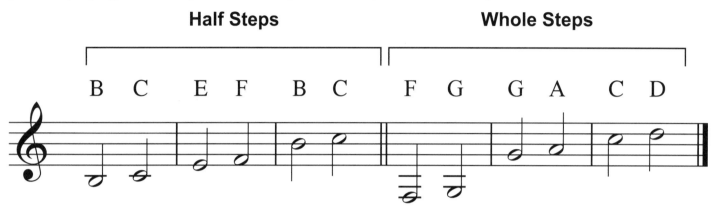

Sharps & Flats

A sharp "#" means higher in pitch by a half step or one fret. A flat "b" means lower in pitch by a half step or one fret. Sharps and flats are used in music when creating chords and scales and are also referred to as accidentals. These symbols are placed before a note on a staff as shown below.

= Sharp
♭ = Flat

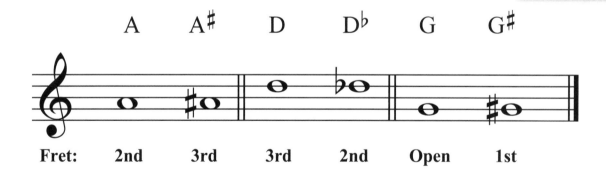

The G Major Scale - Two Octaves

A key signature indicates what notes will be altered within a musical piece. It is a series of sharps or flats found right after the G clef at the beginning of the staff. In the key of "G" all the F notes will be F#. Instead of placing sharp signs before every F note there is an F# at the beginning of every staff. This will tell players that this song is in the key of "G" and that every F will be sharped. Here is what the key signature of G will look like.

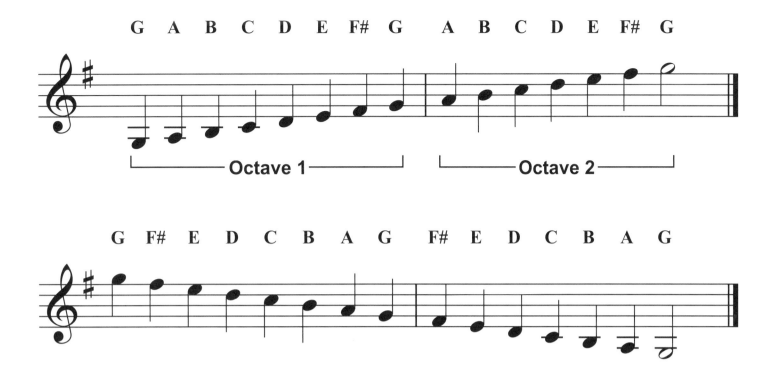

G Major Lead Pattern - Eighth Notes

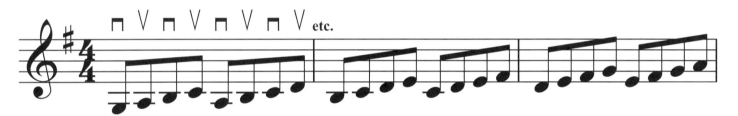

Chords in G Major

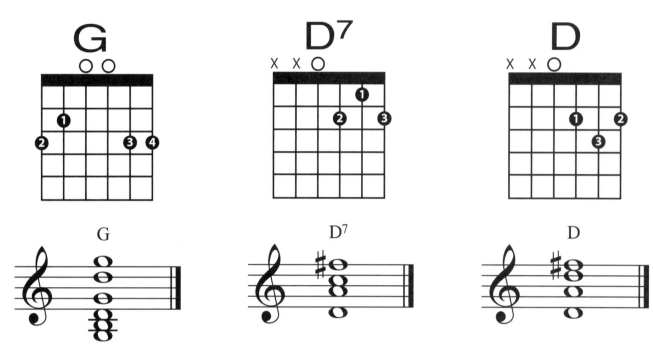

Alternate Strumming

When alternate strumming keep your hand, arm and shoulder relaxed and loose. Pivot the strum from your elbow moving the pick across the strings in a down up motion. Don't strum too far up or down past the strings, keeping a small range of motion. Grip the pick loosely to avoid a stiff sound. Strum pattern 1 is Down – Down – Down Up Down Up. Strum pattern 2 is Down – Down Up – Up Down.

Pattern 1

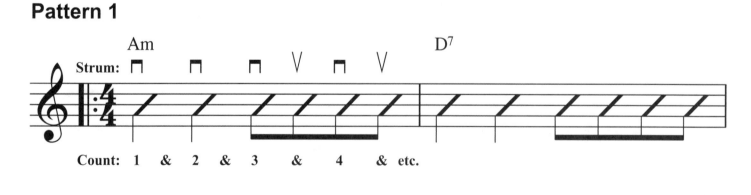

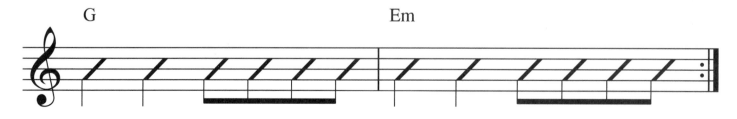

Pattern 2

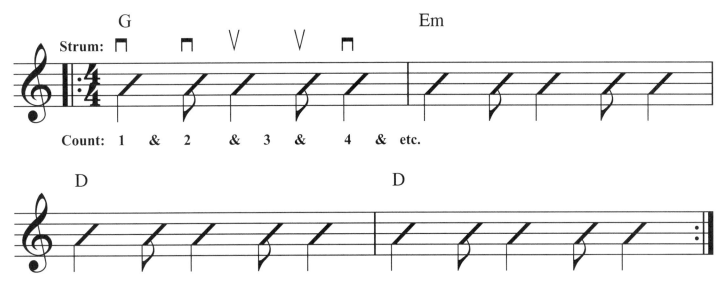

Count: 1 & 2 & 3 & 4 & etc.

G Major Lead Pattern - Triplets

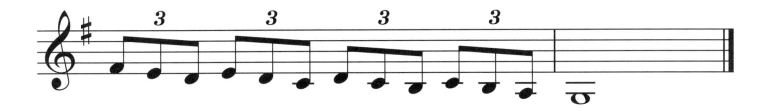

Minuet in G

CD Track 99-100

Andante

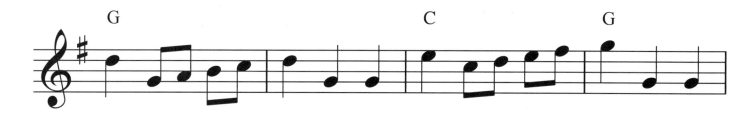

Minuet in G - Rhythm Solo

CD Track 101

Andante

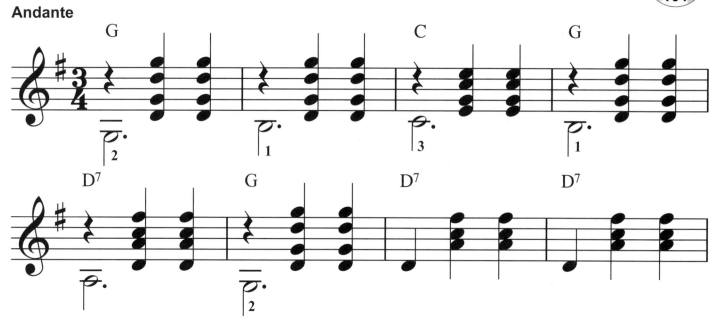

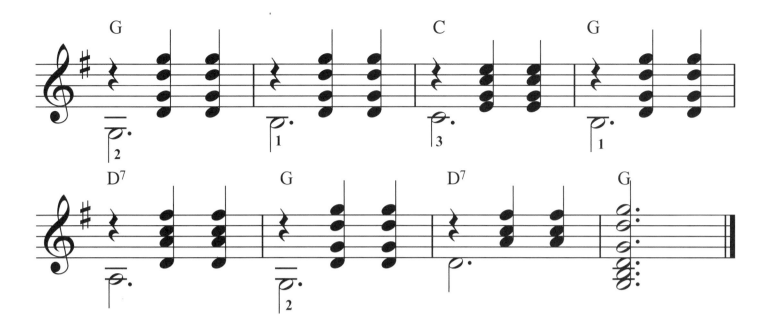

G Boogie Blues

CD Track
102-103

Moderato

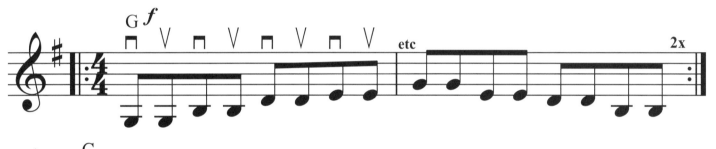

G Major Bass Note Strum

Example 1

Example 2

Adding Your Own Signature to Music

The following song "The Star Spangled Banner" is a well know American patriotic song. This song is sang before most sporting events and special occasions. With a wide range of high a low notes it is known as being a difficult song to sing and many great singers add their own twist to it as they sing by varying the melody or rhythm. Many guitarist also have played unique instrumental versions one of the most well known played by Jimi Hendrix with distortion and feedback. After you learn the standard melody for the song I encourage you to create your own version.

Fermata

A fermata is used to signify that a note should be held longer than the written time value. Exactly how much longer it is held is up to the discretion of the performer or conductor, but twice as long is not unusual. It is usually printed above the note that is to be held longer. Occasionally fermatas are also printed above rests.

The Star Spangled Banner

Andante

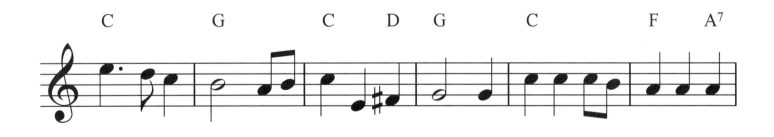

Practice Tips

To ensure constant progress and high motivation you have to develop practice habits that will keep you interested and challenged. Here are a few tips:

Practice Consistently - You need to give your fingers a chance to gain muscle memory. Practice every day even if it is for a short amount of time, be consistent.

Practice Area - Have a practice spot set up so you can have privacy to focus on your playing. It is a great idea to have a music stand to help position your music so you can sit comfortably.

Practice Schedule - Set a scheduled practice time each day and make this a routine. Other times in the day you can play for fun and jam a little.

Finger Flexing #2

CD Track
108

Relative Minor Theory

Every major scale has a relative minor scale that is built starting from the 6th degree. They are called "relative minor" scales because they share the same exact notes. The only difference is the order of the notes. This is a big difference because this changes the tone center and root note which will make it sound like a completely different scale. Below is a C major scale and its relative minor A. As you see, all the notes are completely the same. Just the order is different.

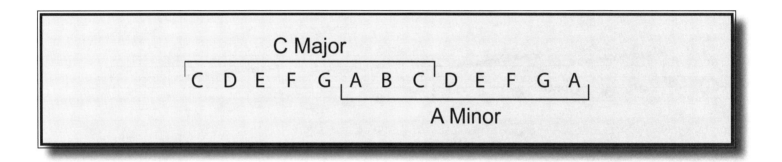

The process of finding the relative minor scale from the 6th degree of the major scale will hold true with any major scale. Be aware that the key signature of both scales will always be the same. For instance, the key of "G" major has one sharp F# so it's relative minor scale E minor will also have the same F sharp note.

The A Minor Scale

Below is the A minor scale. Notice that the notes are the same as its relative C major scale just in a different order. This gives the scale its own tone center and root note A. Play through the scale and listen to how this scale has a sad or minor overall sound. Next, play the C major scale and notice how the same notes have a happy major sound when played in a different order.

Minor Scale Pattern in A

CD Track 109

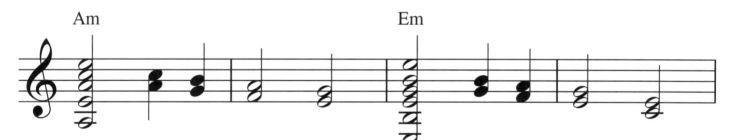

Solo Guitar in A Minor

CD Track 110

Andante

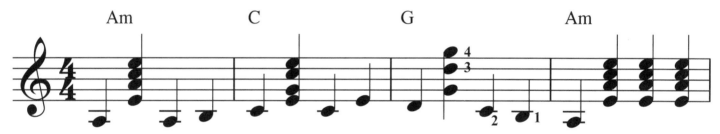

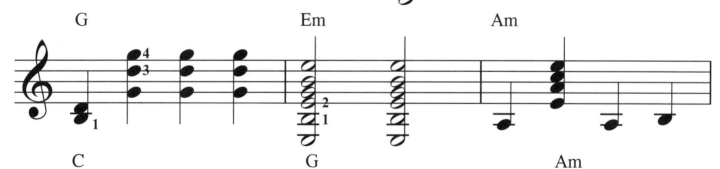

Home on the Range

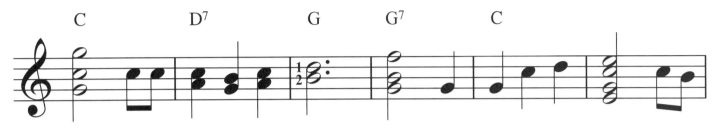

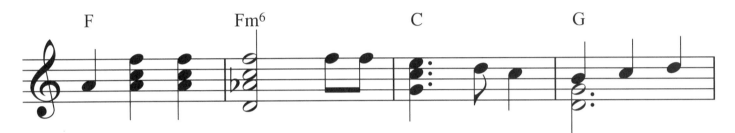

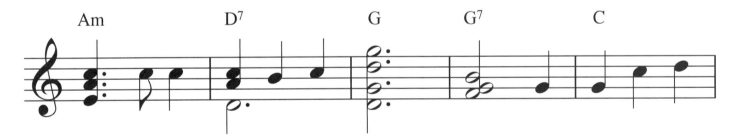

The F Chord

I - IV - V Progression

CD Track 112-113

The 1 – 4 – 5 (or I – IV – V) progression is the most popular chord progression. This chord progression is constructed by building chords off the 1st – 4th and 5th degrees of a major scale. In the key of "C" major C would be the I chord because it is the first note in the scale, F would be the IV chord C – D – E – F and G7 would be the V chord C – D – E – F – G. Many songs in all genres of music have been written using this chord structure so it should sound familiar.

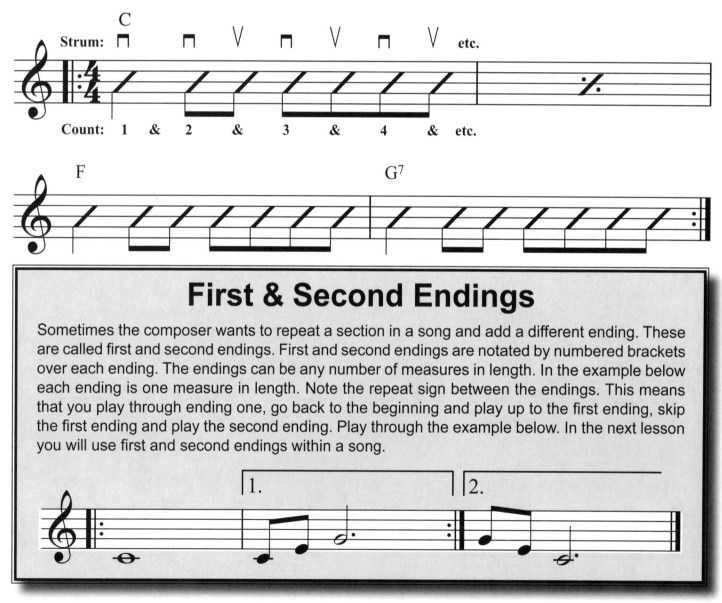

First & Second Endings

Sometimes the composer wants to repeat a section in a song and add a different ending. These are called first and second endings. First and second endings are notated by numbered brackets over each ending. The endings can be any number of measures in length. In the example below each ending is one measure in length. Note the repeat sign between the endings. This means that you play through ending one, go back to the beginning and play up to the first ending, skip the first ending and play the second ending. Play through the example below. In the next lesson you will use first and second endings within a song.

Greensleeves

Andante

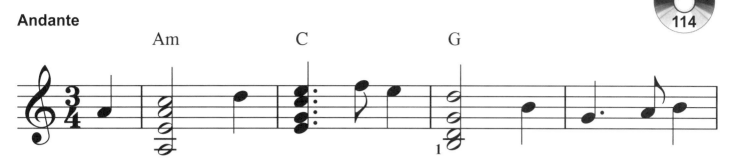

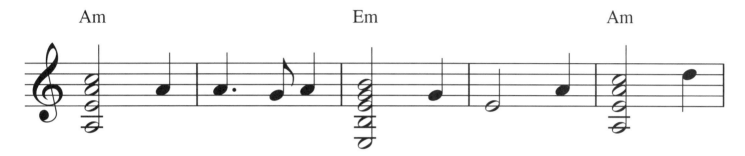

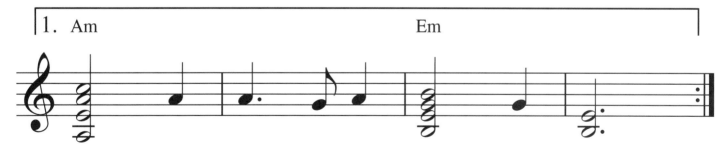

House of the Rising Sun

Hold the chords above the staff for each measure as written allowing the notes to ring.

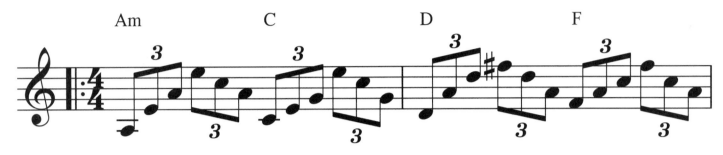

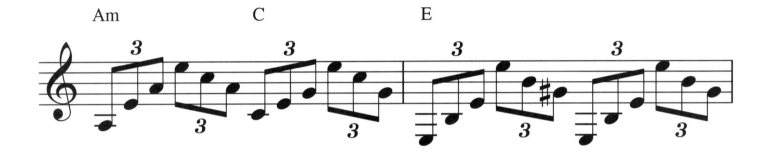

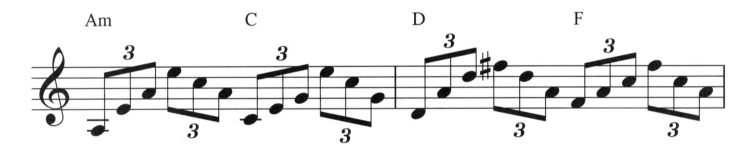

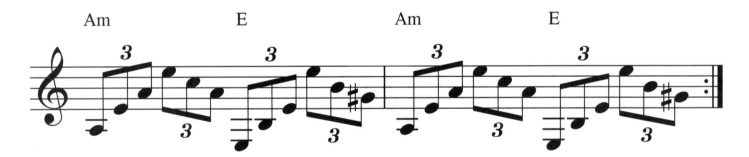

The A Minor Pentatonic Scale - Open Position

The minor pentatonic scale is the most widely used scale in rock and blues music. It is a five note scale that repeats after five scale degrees in a circle type fashion. The notes included in the A minor pentatonic scale are A – C – D – E – G.

Scales are your alphabet for creating leads sund melodies. Just like you learned your alphabet in school and then expanded into words, sentences and complete stories you will learn scales for guitar then expand to melodies, leads and complete songs. Practice the scale on the following page with a metronome and increase you tempo gradually each day.

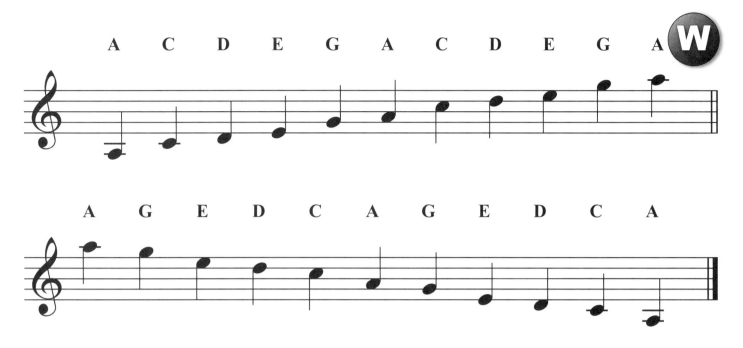

A C D E G A C D E G A

A G E D C A G E D C A

Pentatonic Lead Pattern
Eighth Notes

Pentatonic Lead Pattern - Triplets

Shuffle

The shuffle is a common rhythm feel that has been used by many great guitarists. This uneven rhythm, also called the swing feel, has a bouncy feel that makes your body sway to the music. Play the Pentatonic Lead Melody and the "12 Bar Blues in A" with the shuffle feel. The shuffle feel is notated before a piece of music using the symbol to the right.

Notice to the right how the shuffle is broken down. The first eighth note has the timing equivalence to the first two eighth note triplets on a beat, and the second eighth note gets the last eighth note triplet.

Pentatonic Lead Melody

12 Bar Blues in A

In the 2nd staff there is a B note that will be played on the 3rd string 4th fret instead of open 2nd string as you have played this previously. This is depicted by a circled 3 above the note telling you the string and a 3 next to the note representing the finger.

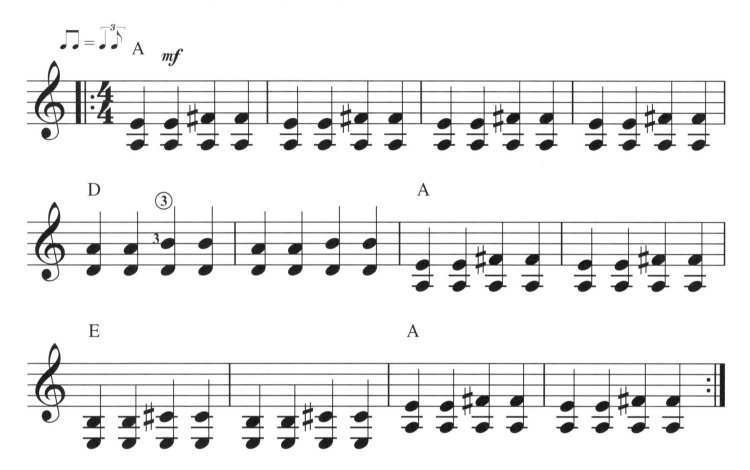

Lead Techniques Bending

Bending is the most widely used technique in modern guitar. It is a great way to add soul and emotional dimension to your notes. To bend a note simply pick it and push your finger up while keeping the pressure pressed down. By doing this you alter and control the note's pitch. A bend will be indicated with two notes connected by an arched line. The first is the note that you fret and the second note tells you what pitch to bend up to. We have also placed a letter "B" above the notes indicating the bend. When fretting the bend keep your other fingers down on the string to help give strength, control and accuracy.

Example 1

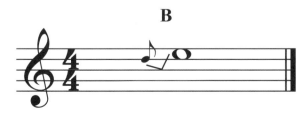

Example 2

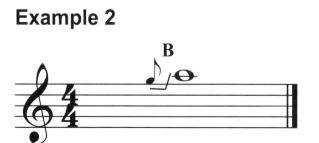

Pentatonic Lead Riffs

Example 1

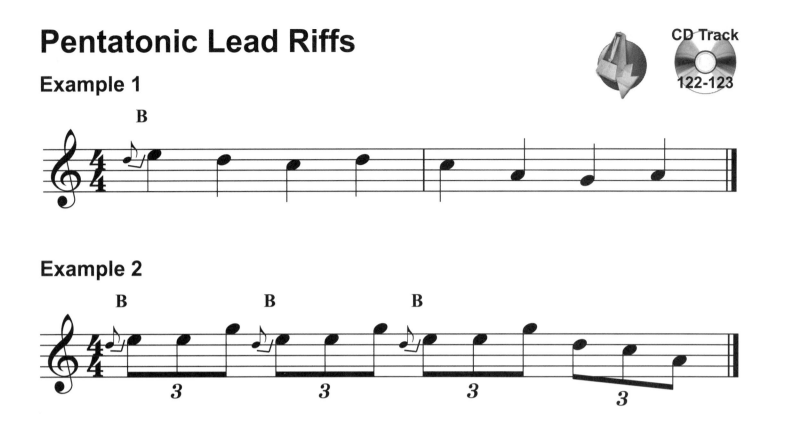

Example 2

The Chromatic Scale

All the music we listen to is derived from a group of 12 notes, all a half step apart, known as the Chromatic Scale. It doesn't matter if it's a complicated classical piece or a simple punk rock song they are all composed using these 12 notes. There are two natural half steps in music: B to C and E to F. There will not be a sharp between these notes.

Natural Half Steps

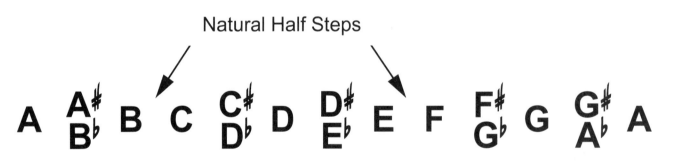

By using this scale and the names of the open strings you can find the name of any note on the guitar. Here is an exercise to see how this works. Start with the open 5th string A note and go up that string one fret at a time following the names of the notes in the chromatic scale as follows: A# 1st fret – B 2nd fret – C 3rd fret – C# 4th fret – D 5th fret and so on all the way up to A at the 12th fret.

Enharmonic Notes

Notice that there is a common flat and sharp note, one note with two different names such as A#/Bb. This is because if you start with an A note and raise it a half step it would be called A#. If you start with a B note and lower it a half step it would be called Bb. Same note, different name. These are called **enharmonic notes**.

The Major Scale Formula

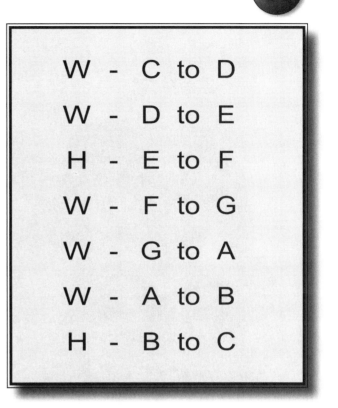

The major scale is the mother of all music. I call it this because most music starts from the major scale. The major scale is constructed using a series of whole steps and half steps. The pattern is: whole step, whole step, half step, whole step, whole step, whole step, half step, or commonly written W – W – H – W – W – W – H. If you start on any note and use this formula you will create a major scale. The starting note will also be the root note (or key). To the right see how the notes of the C major scale follow this formula.

Exercise: As you just learned you can find the name of any note on the guitar using the chromatic scale. Start with the C note on the 5th string 3rd fret and use the formula to the right to play the C major scale all the way up the 5th string.

W	-	C to D
W	-	D to E
H	-	E to F
W	-	F to G
W	-	G to A
W	-	A to B
H	-	B to C

Now let's apply this formula to a few other keys. First the key of "G" major which will have one sharp.

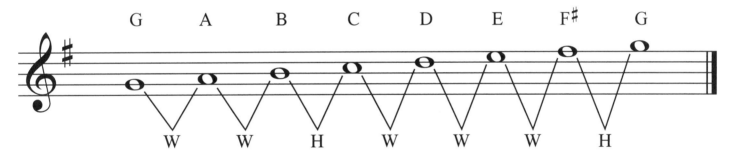

Next apply the formula in the key of "D." This will have two sharps, F# and C# to make the formula work.

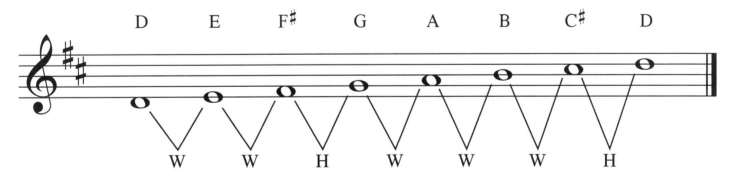

Reading Music for Guitar - Quiz 3
Congratulations you've made it to the end of the program! Go to RockHouseSchool.com and take the quiz to track your progress. You will receive an email with your results and an official Rock House Method "Certificate of Completion" when you pass.

About the Author

John McCarthy
Creator of
The Rock House Method

John is the creator of **The Rock House Method**®, the world's leading musical instruction system. Over his 20 plus year career, he has produced and/or appeared in more than 100 instructional products. Millions of people around the world have learned to play music using John's easy-to-follow, accelerated program.

John is a virtuoso guitarist who has worked with some of the industry's most legendary entertainers. He has the ability to break down, teach and communicate music in a manner that motivates and inspires others to achieve their dreams of playing an instrument.

As a guitarist and songwriter, John blends together a unique style of rock, metal, funk and blues in a collage of melodic compositions that are jam-packed with masterful guitar techniques. His sound has been described as a combination of vintage guitar rock with a progressive, gritty edge that is perfectly suited for today's audiences.

Throughout his career, John has recorded and performed with renowned musicians like Doug Wimbish (who's worked with Joe Satriani, Living Colour, The Rolling Stones, Madonna, Annie Lennox and many more top flight artists), Grammy Winner Leo Nocentelli, Rock & Roll Hall of Fame inductees Bernie Worrell and Jerome "Big Foot" Brailey, Freekbass, Gary Hoey, Bobby Kimball, David Ellefson (founding member of seven time Grammy nominee Megadeth), Will Calhoun (who's worked with B.B. King, Mick Jagger and Paul Simon), Jordan Giangreco from the acclaimed band The Breakfast, and solo artist Alex Bach. John has also shared the stage with Blue Oyster Cult, Randy Bachman, Marc Rizzo, Jerry Donahue, Bernard Fowler, Stevie Salas, Brian Tichy, Kansas, Al Dimeola and Dee Snyder.

For more information on John, his music and instructional products visit RockHouseSchool.com.